GIOVANNA ZOBOLI and **SIMONA MULAZZANI** have collaborated on several previous books, including *I Wish I Had . . .* (Eerdmans), which was awarded the Silver Medal in the Society of Illustrators "The Original Art" 2013 Annual Exhibition. Both of them live in Italy.

Text © 2013 Giovanna Zoboli
Illustrations © 2013 Simona Mulazzani
© 2013 Topipittori, Milano
Translation © Antony Shugaar
Original title: Il grande libro dei pisolini
Topipittori, viale Isonzo 16, 20135 Milan, Italy
www.topipittori.it

Published in 2014 by
Eerdmans Books for Young Readers,
an imprint of Wm. B. Eerdmans Publishing Co.
2140 Oak Industrial Dr. NE
Grand Rapids, Michigan 49505
P.O. Box 163, Cambridge CB3 9PU U.K.

www.eerdmans.com/youngreaders

Manufactured at Tien Wah Press
in Malaysia in October 2013, first printing

19 18 17 16 15 14   9 8 7 6 5 4 3 2 1

Library of Congress Cataloging-in-Publication Data
Zoboli, Giovanna.
[Grande libro dei pisolini. English]
The big book of slumber / by Giovanna Zoboli;
illustrated by Simona Mulazzani;
translation by Antony Shugaar.
pages cm
Summary: "All creatures of the world find time
to rest. And in this lullaby book, countless cozy
animals settle down in their beds"— Provided
by publisher.
ISBN 978-0-8028-5439-1
[1. Stories in rhyme. 2. Bedtime — Fiction.
3. Animals — Fiction. 4. Lullabies.] I. Mulazzani,
Simona, illustrator. II. Shugaar, Antony, translator.
III. Title.
PZ8.3.Z5748Bi 2014
[E] — dc23
2013030890

The Big Book of Slumber

WRITTEN BY
GIOVANNA ZOBOLI

ILLUSTRATED BY
SIMONA MULAZZANI

TRANSLATED BY
ANTONY SHUGAAR

EERDMANS BOOKS FOR YOUNG READERS

GRAND RAPIDS, MICHIGAN • CAMBRIDGE, U.K.

Hushaby, hushaby, such comfy beds.
All of these creatures are resting their heads.

Bears under blankets, lion is snoring.
A twitch of his tail shows he's dreaming he's roaring.

Dolphin and tuna have turned out the light.
Nanny goat's tucking kids in for the night.

Rooster and hen are already sleeping —
so why are those baby chicks still up and cheeping?

Hushaby, lullaby, pillows and sheets.
Cozy young fox is all warm, but her feet.

Doves in the branches and bug on the bark —
only old owl guards them all in the dark.

Crocodile slumbers while counting up sheep.
From frog, toad, and teddy — nary a peep.

Dormouse and badger in beds side by side.
"I like your pajamas," friend badger confides.

Hushaby, hushaby, puppies are sleeping,
while down on the floor two snails come a-creeping.

The camels are snoring in their bunk beds,
with a moonlit oasis right over their heads.

Hippo and sofa are both big and soft,
while doves and seals are asleep high aloft.

In sleeping bags garnished with leaves and boughs,
five giraffes dream of the foliage they browse.

Hushaby, lullaby, turn out the lamp.
Down in the cellar, it's cool and it's damp.

Mouse ate her apple and read her nice book.
Who else is sleeping? Just take a good look.

Snake in his sleep likes to slither and slide.
Coiling and twisting, he dreams he's outside.

In the cupboard the cat won't let go of her ball.
In the drawer right below, moth's asleep in a shawl.

Hushaby, hushaby, beds in the trees.
Bird in her hammock sways soft in the breeze.

Monkey sleeps snug, wrapped in his pajamas,
with no teddy beside him, just his banana.

By tiger's bed there's a bird on a palm.
Both he and zebra are quiet and calm.

All is checkers and stripes, and floral bouquet.
Butterfly's sleepy from such a long day.

Hushaby, lullaby, sleep, stretch, and yawn.
The bunnies are sleeping out on the lawn.

Dormouse sleeps above next to woodpecker neighbors.
Below in the leaves sleep the blackbirds and tapir.

Elephant sleeps on a starry pillow,
and seagull dreams on the tossing billows.

The waves lap away — what a restful sound.
We'll sleep and we'll dream till we reach dry ground.